MonKey Me

AND THE
Pet Show

BY
TIMOTHY RoLAND

BRANCHES

SCHOLASTIC INC.

Read all the **Monkey Me** books!

#1

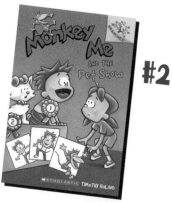
#2

#3

#4

Table of Contents

1: Getting Excited 1

2: Chopper 7

3: Class Picture 11

4: What a Mess! 18

5: Surprise! 28

6: Our Pet Monkey 34

7: Up a Tree 40

8: Pet Show 48

9: Gotcha! 54

10: Pet-Nappers 60

11: What Happened? 66

12: Ready for Action 72

13: Caught! 77

14: Not Again! 84

To Tom, Sue, Pete and Jon, who put
up with (and often encouraged) their
brother's monkey business.
–T.R.

Library of Congress Cataloging-in-Publication-Data Available

ISBN 978-0-545-55981-2 (hardcover) / ISBN 978-0-545-55980-5 (paperback)

Copyright © 2014 by Timothy Roland

All rights reserved. Published by Scholastic Inc.
SCHOLASTIC, BRANCHES, and associated logos are trademarks
and/or registered trademarks of Scholastic Inc.

12 11 10 9 8 7 6 5 4 3 2 1   14 15 16 17 18 19/0

Printed in China   38
First Scholastic printing, April 2014

Book design by Liz Herzog

chapter **1**
Getting Excited

"Slow down, Clyde!" Claudia yelled.

I grabbed a banana off the kitchen table. I stuffed it into my mouth and raced out the front door.

I dashed across my neighbor's front yard. Then I jumped over their flower garden.

Well, almost.

I landed on the last flower . . . or two. I think.
I didn't have time to look back. I had to keep
moving.

"Wait up, Clyde!" Claudia said.

Ha! I ran even faster. I hoped to lose my
twin sister. But two blocks later, she grabbed
my arm.

"Are you crazy, Clyde?" she asked.

"No," I said.

"Or sick?" Claudia asked.

"No." I looked at her. "Why?"

"Because you're never in a hurry to get to school," Claudia said.

"And I'm not today, either," I said.

But I was.

It was class picture day!

Just thinking about it made me excited. And whenever I get excited, I can't stop moving!

"See you later, alligator!" I broke free of Claudia's grip on my arm.

"Oh, no you don't!" She pulled on the back of my shirt and spun me around.

"You need to stay calm," Claudia said.

"Why?" I asked.

Claudia stared. "You know why!"

"No, I don't!" I said.

"Yes, you do!" she said.

"Ha!" I said. "I don't know anything!"

Claudia tried hard not to laugh.

I tried hard to think of something better to say. "Oh, you mean the monkey me."

Claudia nodded. "And it's going to get you in trouble," she said. "Again!"

"Ha!" I said. But I knew my sister was right.

It all started last week at the museum.

Dr. Wally said his experiment changed the banana. He said eating the banana changed the way my body works.

Now I turn into a monkey when I get excited.
Which happens a lot.

"So you need to be careful, Clyde!" Claudia said.

"I will," I said. I began to walk.

"And stay calm!" my sister said.

"No problem," I said.

But I knew it would be.

It was class picture day!

And I was excited!

chapter 2
Chopper

Claudia held onto my shoulders. Then she stepped in front of me.

"Don't worry," I told her. "I'll try to slow down."

My sister's eyes grew large as she spotted something behind me.

"No, Clyde!" she yelled. "RUN!"

I felt the sidewalk behind me shake.

I heard the barking.

And the laughter.

I turned and looked.

"Oh, no!" I yelled. Then I ran as fast as I could in the other direction.

I raced to the nearest tree. I reached for a branch and pulled myself up.

I gasped for air as I looked down at Roz, the class bully. And at Chopper, her bulldog.

"Look what we caught!" Roz said. She pointed at me and laughed.

Chopper barked.

I gripped the tree trunk I was holding even tighter.

Roz is in my class at school and is always picking on me. And now, she had trained her dog to be mean to me, too.

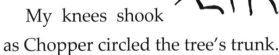

My knees shook as Chopper circled the tree's trunk.

He growled. And grunted. Then he looked up at me and grinned like I was about to become his breakfast.

"Leave Clyde alone!" Claudia yelled. She stepped in front of Roz.

"Or what?" Roz asked.

"Or we'll all be late for school." Claudia glared at Roz.

Roz glared back.

Then Roz looked at me and laughed. "Come on, Chopper!" she said. She put the leash on her dog and pulled.

My knees were still shaking as I watched the growling bulldog leave.

I was afraid of Chopper.

Roz looked at me and yelled, "See you later, little bug!"

I was afraid of Roz, too.

chapter 3
Class Picture

Claudia helped me down from the tree.

"We better hurry," she said. "Or we'll be late for school!"

"And late for the class picture!" I began to run.

The bell rang as I dashed across the playground.

I ran from Claudia and into the school building. I sprinted down the hall and slid around the corner.

"Uh-oh! Principal Murphy!" I slammed on my brakes to try and stop. But I kept sliding.

"Slow down, Clyde!" The principal grabbed my shoulders. She knew me well. I spent a lot of time in her office.

"No running in the building!" Principal Murphy said. "Got it?"

I nodded.

Principal Murphy was carrying a big net. And I knew why. She hoped to catch the monkey she had seen running loose in school.

The monkey me.

Luckily, she didn't know my secret.

Principal Murphy briefly stared at me. Then she continued her search.

When she was out of sight, I continued my running.

I dashed into my noisy classroom and quickly sat at my desk.

"Quiet, class!" Miss Plum said.

The talking stopped.

"I hope you will stay looking this nice until the end of the day," my teacher said, "when we will have our class picture taken."

"I can't wait!" I shouted.

"Clyde!" Miss Plum stared at me.

"Sorry, Miss Plum," I said.

But thinking about the class picture made me bounce. Because I couldn't wait to see who would ruin it this year.

In kindergarten, the Dorney twins stuck their tongues out as the picture was being taken.

In first grade, Roz dropped a worm down Sandy's back. And Sandy screamed just as the man with the camera snapped the picture.

Who's going to ruin this year's picture? I asked myself. It was hard sitting still as I waited to find out.

Finally, at the end of the day Miss Plum led us to the lunch room.

She lined us up in front of the man with the camera. She stood me in the back row on the end next to my sister.

I bounced as I scanned our group.

"Calm down, Clyde!" Claudia whispered.

"I can't," I whispered back.

"Smile!" the man with the camera said.

"And stand still!" Claudia said.

"I'm too excited," I said as I bounced higher.

A wave of energy splashed through me.

My head started spinning. My heart raced.
Faster. And faster.

I sneezed. "A-CHOO!"

chapter 4

What a Mess!

CLYDE!

WHAT'S GOING ON OVER THERE?!

UH-OH! MISS PLUM!

QUICK, CLYDE! SCRAM!

BUT I FORGOT TO SAY "CHEESE."

chapter 5
Surprise!

The school day was over.

And after we sprinted out of the building, I changed back.

"That was close!" Claudia said.

"And fun," I said as I slowed down a little and looked at my body.

I had no monkey hair. Or ears. Or tail.

I was me again!

I quickly dressed.

"Wait up, Claudia!" I yelled. I watched her run farther and farther ahead. She is faster than I am.

But I am trickier.

I cut across my neighbor's lawn and almost beat her to our front door.

Maybe next time.

We raced up the steps and into Claudia's bedroom. She shut the door and sat on her desk chair. I flopped onto her bed.

"Clyde!" she yelled.

I sat up and looked at my sister. She is super neat. Her bedroom is in perfect order.

It's the opposite of mine.

"Stop bouncing, Clyde!" Claudia said.

"I'm not!" But then I looked and saw that I was. And I saw it was driving my sister crazy!

Claudia crossed her arms. "Can't you sit still?"

"Of course I can," I said. I grinned and bounced higher. "I just choose not to."

"Clyde!" Claudia yelled.

I jumped off the bed and grabbed Claudia's doll dressed in a space suit. I raced around the room waving it in the air.

"Clyde!" Claudia yelled.

Claudia plans to become an astronaut and fly to the moon in a rocket. Sometimes, I wish she was already there.

"If you can't behave, Clyde," Claudia said, "then leave!"

"Good idea." I headed toward the door.

"Because I want to look at this." Claudia held up the photo disc.

I quickly stopped. And turned.

I could feel my heart race as I followed my sister to her computer. "I can't wait to see who ruined the class picture," I said.

"You don't know who?" Claudia asked.

"No," I said.

Claudia slid the disc into her computer. The class picture popped onto the screen.

"It was the monkey me!" I said.

Claudia nodded. "So it's good Miss Plum didn't see this picture."

"Or Principal Murphy," I said.

"Or Mom and Dad." Claudia looked to make sure her bedroom door was closed.

"But it is funny." I grinned and pointed to the computer screen. "There's a monkey in our class picture!"

Claudia looked closer and grinned, too.

Then she giggled.

Then, we both laughed. And laughed.

Claudia rolled on the floor. I bounced on her bed. Neither of us could stop laughing, until—

"Claudia? Clyde?"

I spun around and looked. My mouth dropped open. "Mom?"

chapter 6
Our Pet Monkey

"I knocked several times," Mom said. "But I guess you didn't hear me."

"We were . . . busy," I said.

"Yes. Busy," Claudia said. She slowly moved over to block Mom's view of the computer.

"What's so funny in here?" Mom asked.

"Nothing," I said.

"Nothing?" Mom asked.

"You know me," I said. "I like to laugh."

Mom chuckled. "You sure are a giggle box sometimes."

"I am." I grinned.

"But even you don't laugh at nothing, Clyde," Mom said.

She looked at Claudia.

My sister was still standing in front of her computer. Her face turned red.

"Are you hiding something, Claudia?" Mom gently pushed my sister to the side and looked. "That's your class picture on the computer screen, isn't it?"

"Yes," Claudia said. She grabbed Mom's arm. "But you don't want to see it."

"Why not? It looks nice." Mom stared at the computer screen. "I see you, Claudia. But where are you, Clyde?"

I didn't answer. I was hoping she wouldn't notice that I had turned into a—

"Is that a monkey?" Mom asked.

"Uh-oh!" I said.

"What's going on, Clyde?" Mom asked.

I tried to think of an answer she would believe. "It's my pet monkey," I said.

"What?!" Mom said.

"I mean, our pet monkey." I pointed to my sister.

"Is that true, Claudia?" Mom asked.

Claudia looked confused. She has a hard time not telling the truth.

So do I. But sometimes I bend it a little.

"He was loose at school," I told Mom. "And I tried to catch him. But as I did, he jumped into the picture."

Now Mom looked confused. "That's the silliest story you've ever told."

"But it's true, Mom," I said.

"Where's your monkey now?" she asked.

"He likes to stay outside," Claudia said.

"And climb trees," I said.

"And eat bananas," Claudia said.

"Enough with the jokes!" Mom stared. "Just tell me what is going on!"

Claudia looked at me and shook her head no. And she was right.

Who knew what Mom would do if she found out I could turn into a monkey?

"Clyde!" Mom glared at me. "You know the punishment for lying!"

"But I'm not! We do have a pet monkey. And I can prove it!" I raced from Claudia's bedroom and out to the backyard.

I tried thinking about exciting things. Like birthday gifts. The circus. And how a monkey got into our class picture!

I bounced . . . and bounced.

Then my head started spinning. My heart raced. Faster. And faster.

I sneezed. "A-CHOO!"

Up a Tree

chapter 8
Pet Show

"You being a monkey at the pet show could be trouble," Claudia said.

"Ha!" I said. "Trouble is my middle name."

My sister almost laughed. Then she stopped walking. "Maybe we should go home, Clyde."

"But we're almost there," I said. I could see the pet show up ahead.

It was Saturday morning.

Claudia and I stood on the sidewalk and watched people and their pets head into the large building.

I was excited.

And I bounced.

But I had not yet changed into the monkey me. Claudia thought it would be best to wait until later.

"You really think you can win, Clyde?" Claudia asked.

"Of course, once the judges see what I can do," I said. "Like stand on my head. And do flips. And maybe I'll even talk."

"Clyde!" Claudia yelled.

"Just kidding," I said.

"But what if someone finds out your secret?" Claudia asked.

"They won't," I said.

"What if you can't change back from a monkey to a boy?" she asked.

I looked at my sister's worried face.

"We don't know how the change works," she said. "What if something bad happens?"

I paused to think. Claudia is smart and likes to look ahead to what might happen.

But so do I.

"What if everything goes as planned?" I asked her. "And I win? And we finally defeat Roz and Chopper?"

Claudia almost grinned. "But something bad could still happen," she said.

"What are you talking about?" Roz asked as she stepped in front of us. "You're not going to chicken out, are you?"

"No," I said.

Chopper looked at me and growled. He was like a nightmare I wished would go away. Forever!

"So, where's your monkey, Claudia?" Roz looked at me and chuckled. "I mean, your other monkey. The smart one."

Chopper grinned.

Roz laughed harder as she led her dog inside.

We headed into the building. In the huge center room we saw lots of fancy pets.

"Wow!" Claudia said. "Some of these animals must be worth lots of money!"

I looked at a fancy cat.

Then I looked for a place to change. "Come on, Claudia!" I said.

"I'm still worried something bad might happen to you," Claudia said.

"I can't back out now," I said. I sneaked into a side hallway to change.

I thought of exciting things. Like summer vacation! Banana pudding! Defeating Roz and Chopper!

"Is it working?" Claudia asked.

My head started spinning. My heart raced. Faster. And faster.

I sneezed. "A-CHOO!"

chapter 9
Gotcha!

chapter 10
Pet-Nappers

chapter **11**
What Happened?

I was still shaking when I got home. I quickly dressed. Then I poked my head into Claudia's bedroom.

"Clyde! You're alive!" My sister smiled and gave me a big hug. "I was so worried about you!" she said.

I tried to pull away, but couldn't.

"Are you okay?" Claudia asked.

I nodded a little.

"I should never have taken you to the pet show." Claudia hugged me tighter. "Because I knew you would turn into a monkey."

She sat me on the edge of her bed. "And when you turn into a monkey, Clyde, bad things can happen."

"Lots of the owners at the pet show thought they lost their pets," Claudia said. "But I thought I lost my brother!"

My sister's face looked super sad.

For a moment, I looked away from Claudia. At her toys. At her model rockets.

But I didn't feel like playing.

"I searched for you everywhere in the pet show building, Clyde," Claudia said. "So where were you?"

I thought about the warehouse. About the pet-nappers. About escaping from my cage.

I should have been happy.
But I wasn't.

"The show was cancelled," Claudia said. "Because there were so many pets that went missing."

I nodded slowly.

I could see them in my mind, locked in cages in the cold and dark warehouse. They looked hungry. And scared.

"Even Roz was upset," Claudia said. "She was worried about losing Chopper."

I grinned as I thought about my life without the big bully dog. No more running away. Or being trapped up a tree.

It was just what I wanted!

But then
I pictured
Chopper's face
as I raced from
the warehouse.
He looked
scared. Just
like the other
animals.

It made me feel sick.

"Are you okay, Clyde?" Claudia asked.

"Yes," I said. "Why?"

"Because you're sitting still. And you never sit still, unless something's wrong." She leaned closer. "So what is it, Clyde?"

"I was pet-napped and locked in a cage in an old warehouse!" I said.

Claudia's eyes grew wider.

"It was horrible," I said. "And tonight the pet-nappers are planning to sell all the animals!"

Claudia gasped. "Then it's good that you escaped!"

"Yes, it is," I said. "But the other animals are still in danger. And I feel bad about leaving them behind."

Claudia sat on the bed next to me.

"But I don't want to talk about it!" I said.

Claudia placed her hand on my shoulder and smiled. "You just did, Clyde."

"Oh, right," I said. And it felt good getting it out. But it also made me realize what I needed to do next.

Chapter 12
Ready for Action

"This is spooky, Clyde," Claudia said.

We sneaked into the narrow alley behind the warehouse.

It was dark and hard to see.

"Yikes!" Claudia stomped down hard.

OUCH!

"*Oops!* Sorry!" Claudia said.

"You need to calm down!" I said.

"You mean, like you are?" Claudia pointed as I bounced a little.

"Okay, so I'm excited," I said. "It's how I get when I'm ready for action."

I stepped around a box and tried opening the warehouse door. But it was locked.

"How do we get in?" Claudia asked.

"We?" I said. "You're not going in! You're my lookout."

"So I'm here just to watch and warn you if someone comes?" Claudia asked.

"And because you're as worried about the animals as I am." I glanced up at an open window near the top of the warehouse.

73

"So, what's your plan?" Claudia asked.

I grinned. "To turn into a monkey and have some fun."

"Clyde!" Claudia said.

"Okay," I said. "Here it is: My plan is to sneak inside, unlock the cages, and lead the animals to freedom."

"And to be careful," Claudia said.

"Like I always am," I said. I stepped back to look up, and—

"*Oops!*" I looked at the box I tripped over.

"Are you sure you can do this, Clyde?" Claudia helped me to my feet.

"I have to," I said.

Claudia looked worried.

"I'll be fine," I said, "once I change into you-know-what."

"Be careful, Clyde!" Claudia said.

"I will," I said.

I closed my eyes and thought about exciting things. Like skateboarding down the school hallway! Eating a banana split! Freeing the pet-napped animals!

My head started spinning. My heart raced. Faster. And faster.

I sneezed. "A-CHOO!"

OF COURSE HUMANS ARE SMARTER THAN ANIMALS.

THAT'S WHY THE ANIMALS ARE LOCKED IN CAGES.

AND WE HAVE THE KEYS.

chapter 14
Not Again!

On Monday morning the school was buzzing. Everyone was talking about what happened on Saturday.

"Calm down, Clyde!" Claudia said.

"I can't," I said.

My sister grabbed my arm as I tried to run into the school building.

The pet-nappers had been captured. The animals had been freed. And the police said it was because of an unknown hero!

"I wish I could tell everyone it was me," I said to Claudia.

"Don't you dare!" she said. "The principal would know you're the monkey. And catch you!"

Claudia pointed to Principal Murphy carrying her big net down the hallway.

Okay, so I couldn't tell anyone.

But at least I could see the results of what I had done.

The pets were happy. The pets' owners were happy. Even Roz was happy. I think. I hadn't seen much of her that morning.

And that made me happy.

When I got to my classroom, I sat at my desk and bounced. A little.

"Quiet, class!" Miss Plum said. Then she told us to take out our math homework.

"*Oops!*" I said.

"Is something wrong, Clyde?" my teacher asked.

"I forgot to do my homework," I said. "I guess I was too busy last weekend."

Miss Plum stared. "Doing what?"

I had to say something. But I knew I couldn't tell her the truth.

Luckily, just then, Principal Murphy walked into the room. She handed my teacher a note to read.

"The class picture that was taken last Friday is missing," Miss Plum told us.

I looked at Claudia and grinned.

"So today we will be taking a new one," Miss Plum said.

"Yippee!" I yelled.

"And I expect you to behave!" Miss Plum looked straight at me. Then she led my class to the lunch room.

Principal Murphy followed with her big net. "The monkey won't get away this time!" she said.

Miss Plum lined us up just like before.

"And no monkey business, Clyde," Claudia whispered. "Got it?"

I nodded.

"Get ready to smile," the man with the camera said.

I bounced as I tried to see who was going to ruin the picture this time.

"Calm down!" Claudia whispered.

"I can't." I bounced higher.

"Clyde!" Claudia said.

My head started spinning. My heart raced. Faster. And faster.

I sneezed. "A-CHOO!"

Then I heard the camera go *Click!*

Timothy Roland likes monkeys, comics, and monkey comics. That's why he created the Monkey Me book series. He has also written and drawn pictures for a dozen other children's books.

Timothy lives and works in Pennsylvania. He has owned many pets, but never a monkey. If he had one, he might call him Clyde. But probably, he would call the monkey Trouble.

Monkey Me

QUESTIONS & ACTIVITES

CAN YOU ANSWER THESE QUESTIONS ABOUT MONKEY ME AND THE PET SHOW?

Why is Clyde so excited for the class picture?

What does Clyde mean when he says, "I slammed on my brakes"?

Look at the pictures on page 17. What is happening to Clyde?

How does Claudia help capture the pet-nappers?

How does Chopper surprise me at the end of the story?